THE QUICKSAND BOOK

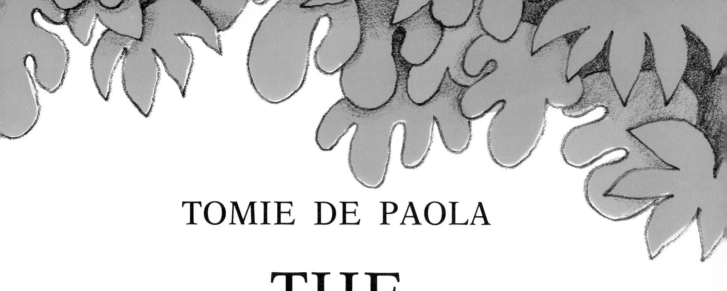

TOMIE DE PAOLA

THE QUICKSAND BOOK

HOUGHTON MIFFLIN COMPANY BOSTON

Atlanta   **Dallas**   **Geneva, Illinois**   **Palo Alto**   **Princeton**   **Toronto**

FOR "STEVEM"
& HIS GRANDMOTHER

Houghton Mifflin Edition, 1991

Printed in the U.S.A.
ISBN: 0–395–55146–3

EFGHIJ–B–998765432

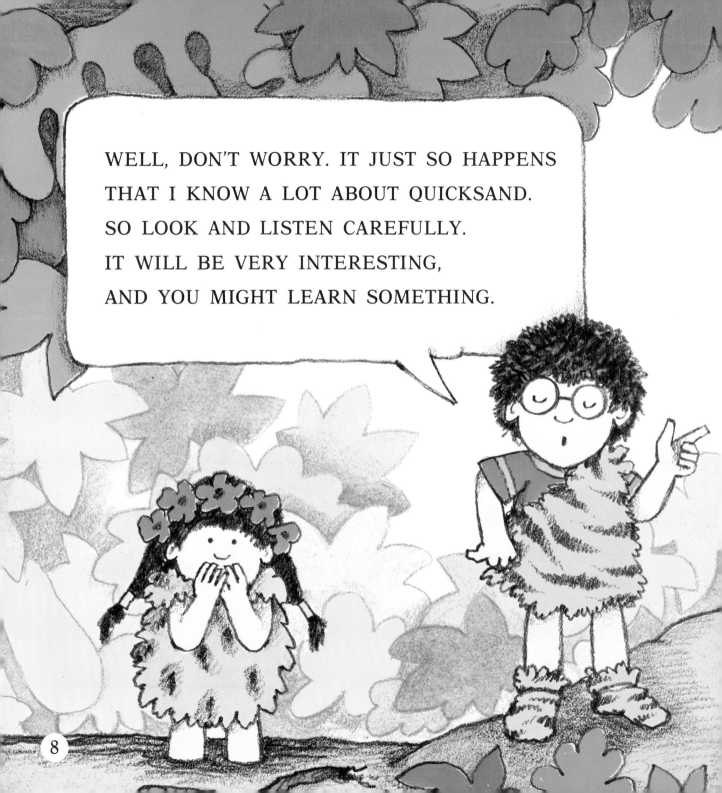

WELL, DON'T WORRY. IT JUST SO HAPPENS
THAT I KNOW A LOT ABOUT QUICKSAND.
SO LOOK AND LISTEN CAREFULLY.
IT WILL BE VERY INTERESTING,
AND YOU MIGHT LEARN SOMETHING.

FIRST OF ALL, QUICKSAND IS NOT A SPECIAL KIND OF SAND. IT IS PLAIN SAND. BUT WHEN WATER IS FORCED UPWARD THROUGH THE SAND, THE GRAINS ARE PUSHED APART AND THE SAND SWELLS. WHEN THIS HAPPENS, THE SAND IS NO LONGER FIRM AND CANNOT SUPPORT HEAVY WEIGHT. THAT IS WHY YOU ARE SINKING.

YOU SEE, WHEN YOU STRUGGLE YOU PUSH MORE
QUICKSAND OUT OF THE WAY AND SINK FASTER.
I'VE NOTICED THAT MOST PEOPLE, IF THEY
STAY CALM, ONLY SINK UP TO THEIR NECKS.
IF YOU HAD FALLEN ON YOUR BACK,
YOU COULD HAVE FLOATED ON TOP OF IT,
THE SAME WAY YOU CAN FLOAT ON THE
GREAT SALT LAKE OR THE DEAD SEA.
BUT IT'S A LITTLE LATE FOR THAT NOW.

EASIER TO SINK

PLAIN WATER

WATER TH LOTS of SALT

WATER WITH LOTS of SAND

EASIER TO FLOAT BECAUSE SALT OR SAND HEL HOLD THINGS UP.

DO YOU KNOW WHERE QUICKSAND CAN BE FOUND? NO? WELL, I'LL TELL YOU. THE MOST COMMON FORM OF QUICKSAND IS FOUND ALONG THE SHORES AND IN THE BEDS OF SLOW RIVERS AND STREAMS THAT HAVE UNDERGROUND SPRINGS, JUST LIKE WHERE YOU ARE.

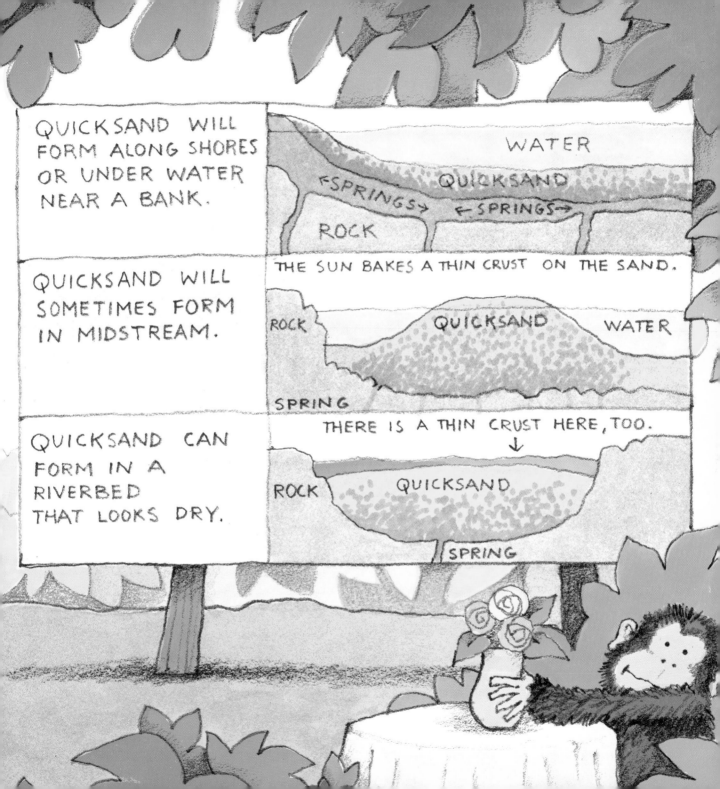

QUICKSAND WILL FORM ALONG SHORES OR UNDER WATER NEAR A BANK.

WATER

QUICKSAND

←SPRINGS→ ←SPRINGS→

ROCK

QUICKSAND WILL SOMETIMES FORM IN MIDSTREAM.

THE SUN BAKES A THIN CRUST ON THE SAND.

ROCK QUICKSAND WATER

SPRING

QUICKSAND CAN FORM IN A RIVERBED THAT LOOKS DRY.

THERE IS A THIN CRUST HERE, TOO.

ROCK QUICKSAND

SPRING

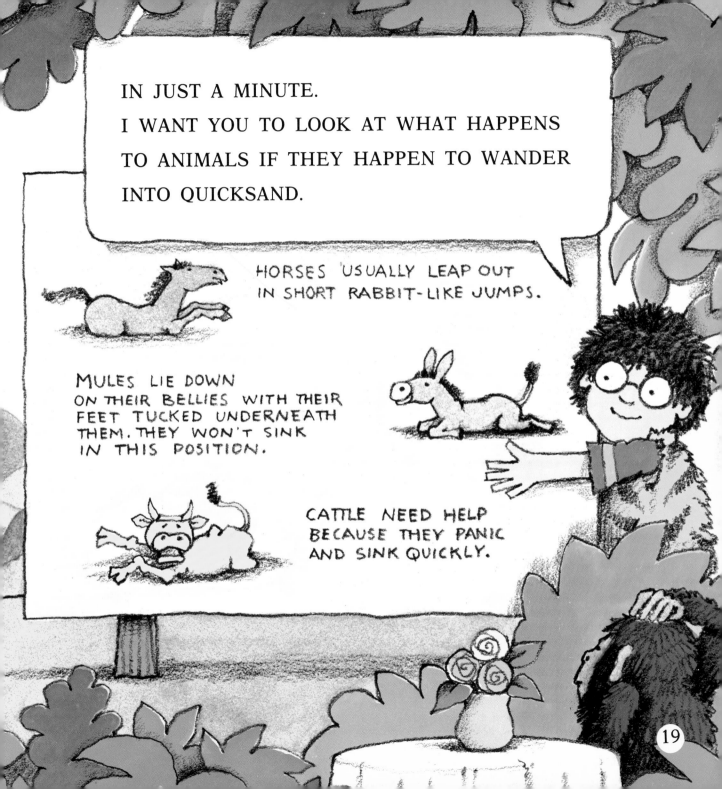

IN JUST A MINUTE.
I WANT YOU TO LOOK AT WHAT HAPPENS TO ANIMALS IF THEY HAPPEN TO WANDER INTO QUICKSAND.

HORSES USUALLY LEAP OUT IN SHORT RABBIT-LIKE JUMPS.

MULES LIE DOWN ON THEIR BELLIES WITH THEIR FEET TUCKED UNDERNEATH THEM. THEY WON'T SINK IN THIS POSITION.

CATTLE NEED HELP BECAUSE THEY PANIC AND SINK QUICKLY.

IF YOU KNEW HOW TO WATCH OUT FOR QUICKSAND, YOU WOULDN'T HAVE FALLEN IN. YOU SHOULD HAVE CARRIED A LONG STICK OR POLE TO TEST THE SAND FIRST. THE QUICKSAND WOULD HAVE ROLLED LIKE WAVES IF YOU HAD DONE THIS.

BUT THE VINE I WAS SWINGING ON BROKE!

24

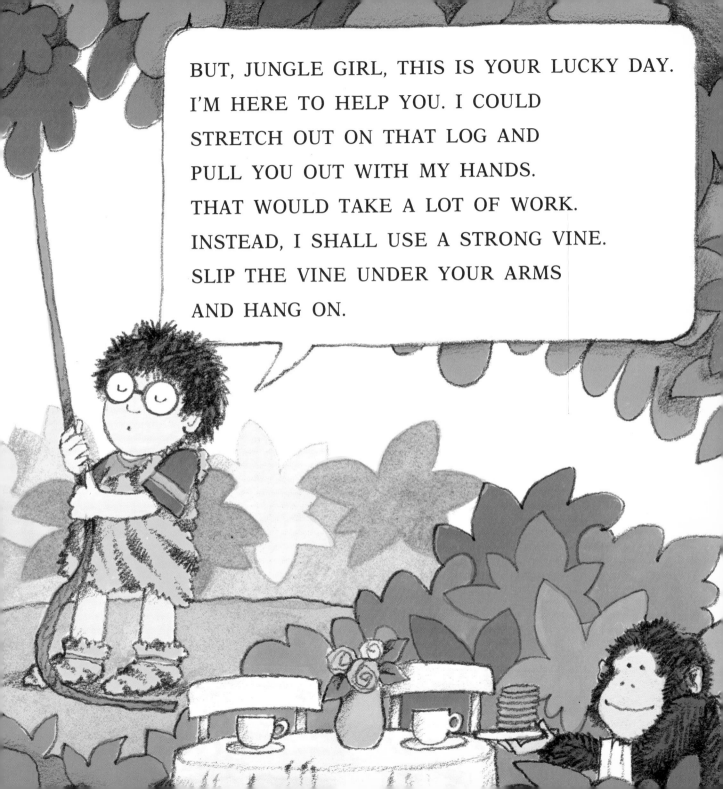

BUT, JUNGLE GIRL, THIS IS YOUR LUCKY DAY.
I'M HERE TO HELP YOU. I COULD
STRETCH OUT ON THAT LOG AND
PULL YOU OUT WITH MY HANDS.
THAT WOULD TAKE A LOT OF WORK.
INSTEAD, I SHALL USE A STRONG VINE.
SLIP THE VINE UNDER YOUR ARMS
AND HANG ON.

How To Make Your Own Quicksand

① MAKE A HOLE IN THE BOTTOM OF A PAIL.

② STICK A HOSE UP THROUGH THE HOLE AND MAKE IT WATERTIGHT.

③ FILL THE PAIL ¾ FULL WITH SAND.

④ PLACE A HEAVY OBJECT ON TOP OF THE SAND. THE OBJECT WILL STAY PUT.

⑤ TURN ON THE HOSE SO THAT A LITTLE WATER TRICKLES UP THROUGH THE SAND. THE SAND WILL SWELL AND GRAINS WILL PULL APART. WHEN THERE IS ENOUGH WATER TO MAKE THE SAND "QUICK", THE OBJECT WILL SINK.

⑥ TURN OFF THE WATER. THE SAND WILL SETTLE AND WATER WILL COME TO THE TOP. THE SAND CAN NOW HOLD ANOTHER HEAVY OBJECT. THIS IS BECAUSE THE WATER IS SQUEEZED TOWARD THE TOP, AND THE GRAINS OF SAND AREN'T PULLED APART AS MUCH.